(continued on back endpapers!)

the LIBRARY BOOK

by **Tom Chapin** and **Michael Mark**

illustrated by **Chuck Groenink**

ATHENEUM BOOKS FOR YOUNG READERS

New York London Toronto Sydney New Delhi

ATHENEUM BOOKS FOR YOUNG READERS
An imprint of Simon & Schuster Children's Publishing Division
1230 Avenue of the Americas, New York, New York 10020
Text copyright © 1989 by HCD Music & The Last Music Co. (ASCAP).
Illustrations copyright © 2017 by Chuck Groenink
Sheet music on endpapers copyright © 1989 by HCD Music & The Last Music Co. (ASCAP). All Rights
Reserved.
For information about special discounts for bulk purchases, please contact
Simon & Schuster Special Sales at 1-866-506-1949 or business@simonandschuster.com.
The Simon & Schuster Speakers Bureau can bring authors to your live event.
For more information or to book an event, contact the Simon & Schuster Speakers Bureau
at 1-866-248-3049 or visit our website at www.simonspeakers.com.
Jacket design by Ann Bobco and Vikki Sheatsley; interior design by Ann Bobco
The text for this book was set in Base Nine.
The illustrations for this book were rendered digitally and in pencil.
Manufactured in China
0717 SCP
First Edition
10 9 8 7 6 5 4 3 2 1
Library of Congress Cataloging-in-Publication Data
Names: Chapin, Tom, 1945– , author. | Mark, Michael L. | Groenink, Chuck, illustrator.
Title: The library book / by Tom Chapin and Michael Mark ; illustrated by Chuck Groenink.
Description: First edition. | New York : Atheneum Books for Young Readers, [2017] |
Summary: Using the lyrics to Tom Chapin and Michael Mark's "Library Song," this picture
book celebrates the magic of reading and of libraries.
Identifiers: LCCN 2016007680 | ISBN 9781481460927 (hardcover) | ISBN 9781481460934
(eBook)
Subjects: LCSH: Children's songs, English—United States—Texts. | CYAC: Libraries—Songs and
music. | Books and reading—Songs and music. | Songs.
Classification: LCC PZ8.3.C366 Li 2017 | DDC 782.42 [E]—dc23
LC record available at https://lccn.loc.gov/2016007680
The song "Library Song" is from the Tom Chapin album *Moonboat*, available for purchase and
download from iTunes and other retailers.

Saturday morning

and the rain is pouring.

Dad worked late last night,  he's in there snoring.

Same old stuff on TV—boring.

So what if I can't go out and play;

I know what I'll do today.

I'm going down to the library,

picking out a book, check it in, check it out.

Gonna
say
hi
to the
dictionary,
picking
out
a book,
check it
in,
check it
out.

Now **I** like books and **they** like me, so when I go to the library,

I sit down in my **favorite chair** and check to see **who's there**.

Maybe **one** book, maybe **two**.

"Take me home,"

says
**Winnie
the Pooh.**
"And
if we have
to travel
far,
I'll bring
my
honey
jar."

Oh, I'm going down to the library, picking out a book, check it in, check it out.

Gonna say hi to the dictionary, picking out a book, check it in, check it out.

Sleeping Beauty **yawned** and **said,**

"I'll come when **I** get **out of bed.**"

But Madeline
says,
"Let her nap!"
and jumps
into
my lap.

The Cat in the Hat says, "Hey, I'll go."

"Don't take him!"
cries Pinocchio.
"Don't take that cat
to your address;
he always makes
a mess."

Oh, I'm going down to the library, picking out a book, check it in, check it out.

Gonna say **hi** to the dictionary, picking out a book, check it in, check it out.

Mrs. Parker's
back behind the checkout desk today.
The Cheshire Cat jumps on her head
and says,

"Let's play!"

But Mrs. P. says,
"Goodness,
are you sure
you want all these?"

"oh yes!"
we shout together.

She says . . .

"Shhh! Quiet, please!"

I'm going down to the library, picking out a book, check it in, check it out.

Gonna say hi to the dictionary, picking out a book, check it in, check it out.

The Seven Dwarfs begin to shout,
"Say,
take us with you.

Check
us
out!"

Then Cinderella
gets her
gown
and
Babar
grabs his
crown.

Then Curious George swings from the shelf.

Along comes Mother Goose herself.

Out the door we danced and sang.

The whole library rang.

Gonna say **hi** to the dictionary, picking out a book, check it in, check it out.

Picking out a book, check it in, check it out!

(continued from front endpapers!)